ORINDA

D0600650

The Wonderful Thing About Hiccups

To my wonderful family,
Erika, Alex, and Lee
—C. M.

For every librarian
who has helped me
find whatever I was
searching for
—J. P.

THE WONDERFUL THING ABOUT HICCUPS

BY Cece Meng

ILLUSTRATED BY Janet Pedersen

Clarion Books ■ New York

T he wonderful thing about hiccups is that they make people laugh. I noticed this during story time at the library. Libraries are ordinarily quiet places.

The wonderful thing about quiet places is that they make loud hiccups sound even louder.

Hiccup!

Hiccup!

Hiccup!

My little sister says that very loud hiccups sometimes go away when you hang upside down and drink water.

You are not allowed to do this in the library, though.

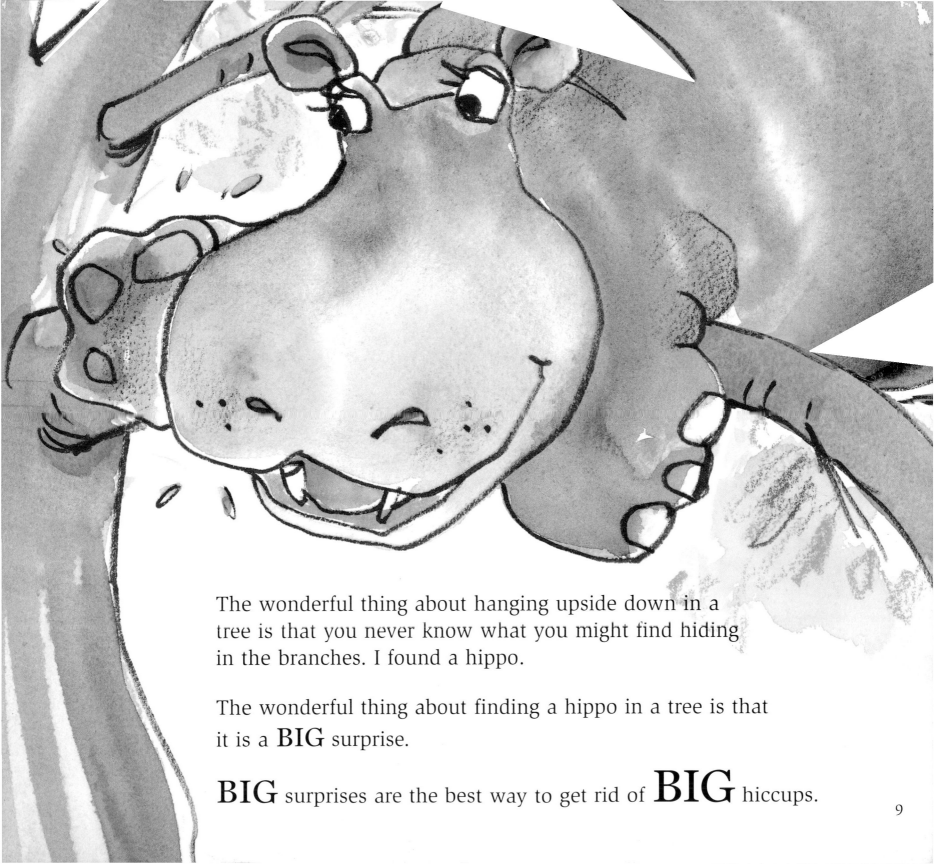

The wonderful thing about hanging upside down in a tree is that you never know what you might find hiding in the branches. I found a hippo.

The wonderful thing about finding a hippo in a tree is that it is a **BIG** surprise.

BIG surprises are the best way to get rid of **BIG** hiccups.

Hippos are the best way
to carry your library books.

The wonderful thing about having a hippo
carry your library books is that he can hold
them high enough so they will not get wet in
the sprinklers. Little sisters, on the other hand,
get wet quite easily.

11

The wonderful thing about little sisters is that they dry off quickly when your hippo blows and blows and blows.

It is not so wonderful when your library books blow away.

12

The wonderful thing about flying
books is that they eventually land.

There is nothing wonderful about having them land in a yard with a giant dog. I suggest having a giant hippo there to help you.

Though holding on to library books while riding a scared, running hippo is hard.

The wonderful thing about dropping library books while riding a scared, running hippo is that hippos are good at catching them before they fall into the dirt.

Little sisters, on the other hand, fall into the dirt quite easily.

There is nothing wonderful about an angry little sister. Especially when her yelling scares your hippo right into an ice cream cart.

Flying ice cream is a wonderful way to share with everyone in the neighborhood.

Library books do not make wonderful plates.

The wonderful thing about having an ice cream party is that you get to watch the hippo eat ten scoops in a row. Do not let him hold your library books while doing this, though. He may accidentally swallow them.

There is nothing wonderful about swallowed library books.
There is nothing wonderful about a hippo with a bellyache.

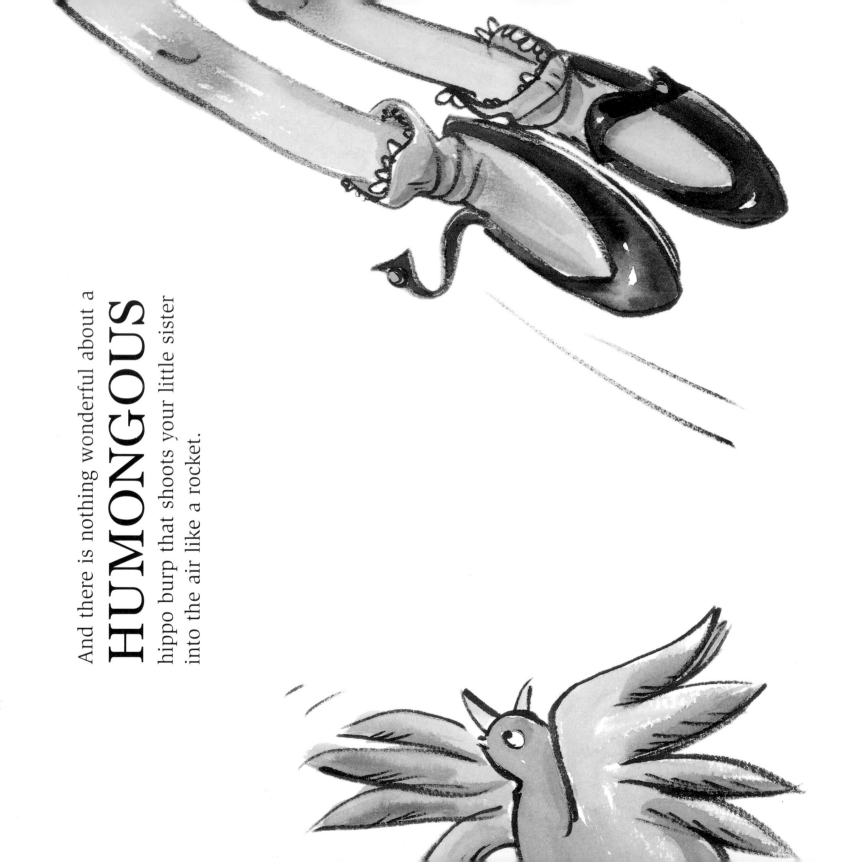

And there is nothing wonderful about a **HUMONGOUS** hippo burp that shoots your little sister into the air like a rocket.

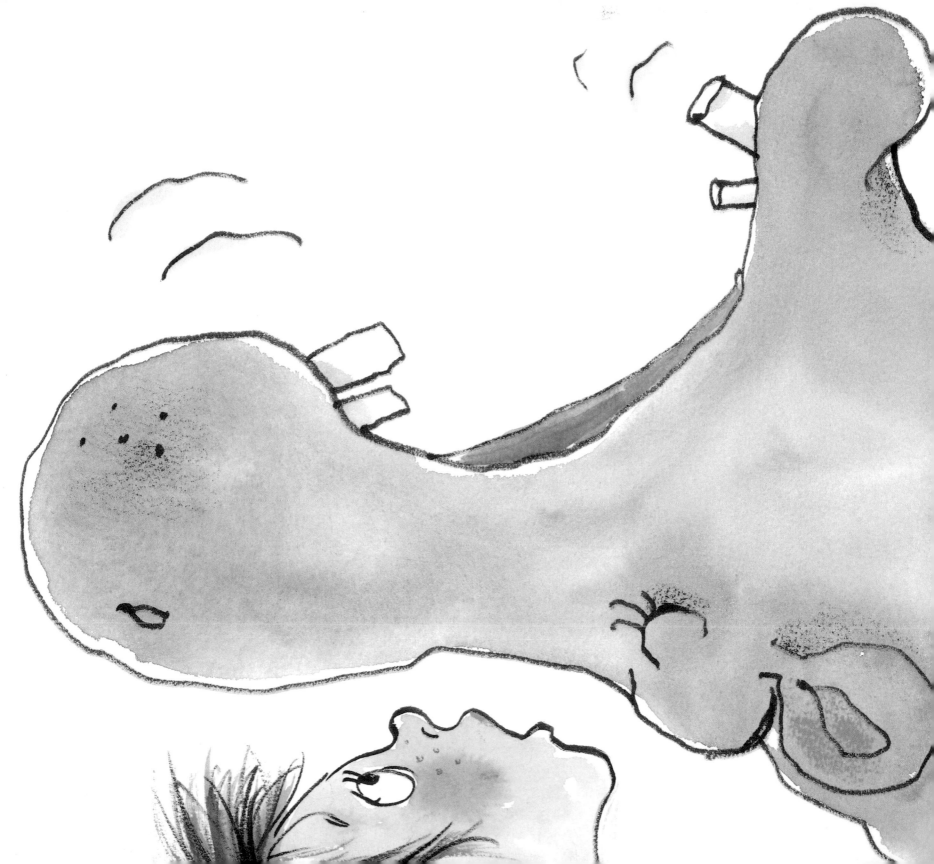

Standing on a hippo is a wonderful
way to look for a little sister.

It is not so wonderful when you have to explain to the librarian why your little sister is stuck on the roof of the library.

23

The wonderful thing about
librarians is that they are
great at rescuing little sisters.
Some librarians may forget to tell
you they are afraid of high places.

Jumping down from high places is wonderful only if you use a hippo belly as a landing cushion.

The wonderful thing about belly bouncing on
a hippo is that, if you are lucky, you just may
bounce your library books right out of his mouth.

The wonderful thing about getting library books back is that you finally get to read them. Hippos are great listeners, though they may ask you to read their favorite book over and over and over.

Finished library books
are to be returned on time.

The wonderful thing about returning your books to the library on time is that you can prove to your mother that you really **ARE** ready for your very own library card.

And what's so wonderful about that?

29

If your hippo gets the hiccups during story time,
you just may find the cure in a book.

Hic!

ᔕ LIBRARY BOOK RULES TO REMEMBER ᔕ

ᔕ Do not get books wet. As in, keep them out of sprinklers, rainstorms, swimming pools, bathtubs, and definitely the toilet.

ᔕ Only books with wings, books shot from cannons, books on rocket ships and airplanes, or books belonging to space aliens are allowed to fly.

ᔕ Keep them out of the dirt and away from mean dogs.

ᔕ Do not eat strawberry ice cream, noodles, fresh broccoli, birthday cake, or any other kind of food off them.

ᔕ Do not feed them to strange animals.

ᔕ Do not feed them to your little sister.

ᔕ When you are done, return them to the library so you can check out more books. Do not return them to the grocery store, pet store, or toy store. *Never* return them to space aliens.

ᔕ Always thank librarians. (You never know when you may need their help.)

Clarion Books
a Houghton Mifflin Company imprint
215 Park Avenue South, New York, NY 10003
Text copyright © 2007 by Cece Meng
Illustrations copyright © 2007 by Janet Pedersen

The illustrations were executed in pen, watercolor, and crayon.
The text was set in 16-point ITC Slimbach.

www.clarionbooks.com

Manufactured in China

Library of Congress Cataloging-in-Publication Data

Meng, Cece.
The wonderful thing about hiccups / by Cece Meng ; illustrated by Janet Pedersen.
p. cm.
Summary: A bad case of hiccups in the library leads to a series of outlandish experiences and
a set of rules related to library books, hippopotamuses, and little sisters.
ISBN-13: 978-0-618-59544-0
ISBN-10: 0-618-59544-9
[1. Books and reading—Fiction. 2. Hippopotamus—Fiction. 3. Sisters—Fiction.
4. Hiccups—Fiction. 5. Humorous stories.] I. Pedersen, Janet, ill. II. Title.
PZ7.M5268Won 2007
[E]—dc22
2006006270

WKT 10 9 8 7 6 5 4 3 2 1